Just Baby Fat

by
J.D. PARKS

You are a ray of sunshine in the darkest class. Thank you!

Parks Publishing Company, LLC

Paperback: 978-1-7326967-9-2

First paperback edition August 2021

Edited by J.D. Parks
Cover art by Blackk_arts

Parks Publishing Company, LLC
P.O. Box 66
Olive Branch, MS 38654

jdparks.com

This book belongs to

_____

Dedication

To all who have been told, "It's just baby fat" and walked away loving themselves even less than before.

My new shoes squeaked loudly against the freshly waxed floor. My teacher stood smiling and waving at the door.

"Ah, come in! What is your name?"

"Mimi!" I exclaimed. "Or Michelle Renée James!"

"Welcome, Michelle! Give me your hand and let me show you your desk."

"Ooh, look at her big belly in that dress," one girl began to jest.

"It's jiggling and bouncing everywhere!" another boy said.

"Yeah, she can't be our friend," the girl laughed, her face turning red.

I slid into my desk, trying hard not to cry. But it didn't work; so, I used my shirt sleeve to wipe my face dry.

Then, it was time for lunch, so I got in the line.

Once I got to the front, the lunch lady said, "Here, sweetheart, try a salad this time."

"Why?" I asked, staring down at my tray.

She put her hands on her hips and said, "A salad a day keeps the baby fat away."

With my head hanging low, I sat down to eat, but none of my classmates would even talk to me.

"Ms. Harvey!" I yelled, running after my teacher at the end of the day. "Today at recess, I didn't get to play."

"Why not?" she asked. "I don't like hearing that."

"They all said that I'm too fat."

She grabbed my hands and said, "It will all get better day by day. It's just baby fat; one day, it will all go away."

"It will?!" I squealed, jumping up and down.

"I promise," she said, picking me up and twirling me around.

I woke up the next day, ready to see all the weight that had fallen off me, but standing in front of the mirror, my tears started to flow. I was still fat, and my belly was hanging low.

"Mimi!" Mama yelled. "Come and eat breakfast before you and daddy have to go!"

"I want to Mommy, but my stomach says no!"

"Pumpkin, what's wrong?" Daddy asked, lifting my chin.

"I'm not really hungry, and I want to make friends."

"Sweetheart, you'll make friends," he said. "But you have to eat."

"Not if I want my baby fat to leave."

"Baby fat?" Mama asked, shaking her head. "Where did you learn that?"

"At school," I replied. "All the kids say that I'm fat."

"And when you told your teacher, what did she say?"

"She said that one day it will all go away, but look at me! Why didn't it happen today? The lunch lady gave me a salad yesterday."

"I know that their words hurt you, and Mommy and Daddy are sorry they made you feel this way," Mama said. "You're beautiful no matter your size."

"Especially," Daddy said, "When I look in your eyes, but what's more important is that your heart is beautiful, too."

"Daddy's right. God knew what HE was doing when HE made you. Even if you get more belly or grow very tall, real friends will like you through it all.

"So, what should I do when people call me fat?"

"Raise your head up high, way up to the sky," Daddy said, "and then, turn around and walk away, and repeat the same steps every day."

"And when their words hurt, "Mama said, "remember that GOD did not want everyone to be the same, and you're beautiful because you were made in His name."

"So, look in the mirror and say, 'I love you,' and guess what? Mommy and Daddy love you, too."

THE END.

A Prayer for Me

As I close my eyes to sleep,
I pray to GOD to see about me.
To hug me tight and hold me close,
To love me like no one else knows,
To help me love myself more every
day and to teach others to love the
same way.

Amen.

Want more J.D.?

Leave a review on Amazon!

Visit www.jdparks.com to join the email list
or email J.D. at: contact@jdparks.com

Follow J.D.!

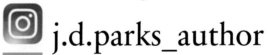 j.d.parks_author

DrJalesaParks

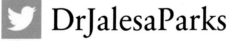 DearJDParks